THE ART OF BEING A WANKER

Master the Fine Craft of Everyday Annoyance

Sir Knobulous W. Pompington

Hennen Publishing

Copyright © 2025 Sir Knobulous W. Pompington

All rights reserved. No part of this book may be reproduced, redistributed, or used as toilet paper without the prior written permission of the publisher, except in cases of mild emergencies (or if you're Barry from accounting—seriously, Barry, you owe us an apology).

Published by: Hennen Publishing
For complaints, love letters, or inappropriate memes:
hennen.publishing@gmail.com
Cover design by Marwood

First Edition, 2025

Printed in the United Kingdom by someone who probably questioned all their life choices while handling this masterpiece.

Legal Disclaimer: This book is for entertainment purposes only. Any resemblance to actual wankers, living or dead, is purely coincidental. If you think this book is about you, it probably is. Don't sue us; we're broke.

ISBN: 9798303406490 Hardcover

Sir Knobulous W. Pompington
The Art of Being a Wanker

1. Humour – 2. Self-Help (but not really) – 3. Absolute Nonsense

Printed on paper that's probably recyclable.
Please do your bit for the planet—unless you're too much of a wanker to care.

*To all the wankers out there—
The ones who clap when the plane lands, hog the middle lane,
and talk endlessly about their "personal brand."
You are the unsung heroes of chaos, the architects of minor
inconveniences, and the reason group chats descend into
anarchy.
This book is for you. Never change.*

*Yours in glorious wankery,
Sir Knobulous W. Pompington*

Wanker (noun):
/ˈwæŋ.kər/ (British slang, informal)

Literal Meaning: A vulgar term referring to someone who engages in self-gratification, often used as an insult to imply self-centredness or idiocy.

Colloquial Use:

A person who is arrogant, self-absorbed, or irritating in their behaviour.
Someone who makes a big deal out of trivial matters, often acting superior, obnoxious, or clueless in social situations.
The person in a group who insists on saying "ciao" instead of goodbye or corrects someone's pronunciation of "bruschetta" even though they don't speak Italian.

Characteristics of a Wanker:

Overconfident with little reason to be.
Fond of unnecessary drama or attention-seeking behaviour.
Often the self-proclaimed expert in a subject nobody cares about.

Example Sentences:

"Did you see Greg post another selfie with the caption 'Rise and grind'? What a wanker."
"The guy at the bar just ordered a craft beer flight and started lecturing the bartender about hops. Absolute wanker."

"Life is a game, and wankers are just here to change the rules, forget the rules, and then blame someone else for it."

SIR KNOBULOUS W. POMPINGTON

CONTENTS

Title Page
Copyright
Dedication
Epigraph
Preface
Introduction

Wankers at Work	1
The Art of Being an Everyday Wanker	7
Romance for Wankers	12
Wanker on the Town	17
Wanker Wisdom	21
Wankers Unite	26
Wanker at Home	30
The Existential Wanker	35
Wankers of the World	40
Wanker Fitness	45
Wanker Parenting	50
The Seasonal Wanker	55
Wanker at the Wheel	60
Afterword	65
A Note on the Cover Design	67

Praise For Author

PREFACE

"An Ode to Wankers"

Every so often, a truly revolutionary book comes along. A book that changes lives, reshapes minds, and challenges society to think differently.

This isn't that book.

This is a book about wankers—unapologetic, irrepressible, and delightfully infuriating wankers. The kind who double-dip hummus at parties, insist on saying *"ciao"* when leaving the office, and loudly announce their CrossFit times without being asked.

The world needs wankers. We're the ones who keep things interesting, whether by sending a cryptic *"we need to talk"* text to spice up someone's day or turning a simple brunch into a three-hour Instagram photoshoot. Without us, life would be as dull as a beige wall in an empty office cubicle.

This book isn't about *how* to be a wanker—you're already doing that just fine. It's about celebrating the art of wankery, leaning into your quirks, and finding joy in being just a little bit annoying. So, if you've ever felt guilty about being that person, let this book be your absolution.

Unapologetically yours,
Sir Knobulous W. Pompington

INTRODUCTION

"The Fine Art of Wankery"

Let's face it: life is far too short to take seriously. It's also far too long to spend pretending you don't occasionally clap when a plane lands, hog the armrest at the cinema, or insist that oat milk is better than regular milk (it's not, but we'll die on that hill).

If you've ever corrected someone's grammar mid-conversation, used a cryptic Facebook status to fish for attention, or sent an unnecessary *"per my last email,"* congratulations—you're one of us. A proud, unapologetic wanker.

This book isn't here to judge you. Quite the opposite. It's a celebration of everything gloriously irritating about being alive: the pettiness, the chaos, and the sheer joy of being the human equivalent of Marmite—loveable to some, utterly intolerable to others.

Inside these pages, you'll find practical advice (of questionable quality) on how to dominate every arena of life with your unique blend of arrogance, wit, and total disregard for other people's patience. Whether you're sending passive-aggressive texts, ruining group chats, or asserting your dominance in the gym, this guide will help you embrace your inner wanker and take your twattery to new heights.

So, buckle up. Whether you're here for a laugh or a lesson (or both), this book is your permission slip to lean into life's absurdities with gusto. Just remember: if nobody's rolling their eyes at you, are you even trying?

Let's dive in...

WANKERS AT WORK

Chapter One

*"Bullshit Bingo and Other
Corporate Survival Tactics"*

The workplace: a maze of passive-aggressive emails, pointless meetings, and Ben from IT who somehow always smells like wet cardboard. Whether you're aiming to climb the corporate ladder or just survive another soul-sucking Monday, this chapter will teach you how to dominate the office as the glorious wanker you were born to be.

1. Buzzwords and Bullshit:

The secret to surviving any workplace is mastering the art of saying absolutely nothing in as many words as possible. Corporate jargon is your best friend here. The more meaningless, the better.

Top Wanker Buzzwords to Use Liberally:

"Let's touch base."
(Translation: I'm about to waste 15 minutes of your life.)
"Low-hanging fruit."
(Translation: I'm lazy, and you're doing this.)
"Circle back."
(Translation: I forgot to do my job, so let's talk about it again later.)

"Value-added."
(Translation: We're charging more for the same shit.)

Pro Tip: Throw in words like *"synergy"* and *"paradigm"* randomly, even if they make no sense.
Example:
  "I think we need to leverage our core competencies to create a game-changing paradigm shift."
Congratulations, you've said nothing at all, and everyone's nodding.

2. Passive-Aggressive Email Olympics:

Why say, *"You're an idiot,"* when you can say, *"Per my last email..."*? The key is to sound polite while radiating utter contempt.

Examples of Elite Email Wankery:

  "Just circling back on this—didn't want it to slip through the cracks!"
  (Translation: Do your bloody job.)
  "Let me know if there's anything I can clarify!"
  (Translation: You're too stupid to understand the first time.)
  "Happy to help!"
  (Translation: I'll burn this fucking building down if you email me again.)

Advanced Move: CC the boss unnecessarily. Nothing says *"power move"* like dragging your manager into a minor dispute over stapler placement.

3. Meetings That Should Have Been Emails:

We've all been there. You're stuck in a two-hour meeting about quarterly projections that could have been summed up in a three-sentence email. The key to surviving these? Talk without saying anything.

Tips for Meeting Domination:

> Repeat the last thing someone said, but slower.
> *"What I'm hearing is… revenue alignment across touch points."*
> Everyone will nod like you're a genius.
> Ask vague questions like, *"What's the ROI on this?"* Nobody knows. Nobody ever knows.
> Volunteer for something vague and non-committal: *"I can lead the brainstorming session."* You'll never have to do it.

Advanced Wanker Move: Bring a notebook. Write *"blah blah synergy"* repeatedly while nodding thoughtfully. Occasionally furrow your brow like you've just had an epiphany.

4. Lunchroom Shenanigans:

Microwave fish. It's the ultimate *"fuck you"* to everyone else in the office. Bonus points for loudly saying, *"Mmm, smells so good!"*
Steal someone else's clearly labeled lunch, then blame it on Barry from accounting.
Spend 20 minutes loudly discussing your keto diet. Nobody asked, nobody cares.

Advanced Move:
Leave the microwave door open with food splattered everywhere. Deny responsibility.

5. Wanker Pro-Tips:

Desk Decor: Add motivational quotes like, *"Dream Big"* or *"Hustle

Hard." You've cried into your keyboard three times this week.

The Power Point: Always point aggressively during presentations. Doesn't matter if you're pointing at nothing—confidence is key.

Toilet Politics: Use the cubicle as your personal podcast studio. Have loud phone conversations. Flush mid-call for dominance.

6. The LinkedIn Wanker:

LinkedIn is your stage, and you are the star of this absolute shitshow. Post cringeworthy updates like:

> "Humbled to announce I've been promoted to Senior Paperclip Organiser."
> "Monday Motivation: Remember, YOU are the architect of your success."
> A 500-word essay about how stapling papers taught you the value of teamwork.

> ***Advanced Wanker Challenge: The Corporate Bullshit Bingo***
> *Print this out and tick off as many buzzwords as you can during your next meeting:*
> - *Touch base*
> - *Low-hanging fruit*
> - *Circle back*
> - *Game-changer*
> - *Out-of-the-box*
>
> *If you get a full row, shout, "BINGO!" and walk out.*

7. Desk Wars

Your desk isn't just a workspace; it's a battleground for dominance.

How to Establish Your Territory:

Overdecorate: Cover your desk in motivational quotes like *"Hustle Hard"* and *"Dream Big."* Bonus points for adding a Himalayan salt lamp "to balance the energy."
Snack Tyranny: Keep the smelliest snacks in your drawer—think tuna, boiled eggs, or garlic hummus. Enjoy them with gusto during meetings.
Stationery Hoarder: "Borrow" pens, staplers, and scissors from coworkers. When they ask for them back, act deeply insulted.

Advanced Move:
Bring in a standing desk. Mention it in every conversation. *"Oh, I just feel so much more productive standing."*

4. The Zoom Wanker

Remote work hasn't dulled the shine of wankery—it's given it new platforms to thrive.

How to Be the Worst on Zoom:

The Background Bragger: Use a tropical beach or a library full of leather-bound books. Insist it's *"authentic."*
Mic Unmuted: Leave your mic on while typing loudly or shouting at your dog. Bonus points for accidentally playing *Baby Shark* in the background.
The Overzealous Nodder: Constantly nod dramatically during meetings as if you're deeply invested.

Advanced Move:
Show up in a blazer with pyjama bottoms. Forget to turn off your camera when you stand up.

Conclusion: How to Win at Work Without Really Trying

Being a workplace wanker isn't just about surviving the grind—it's about thriving in the chaos. With the right buzzwords, passive-aggressive emails, and fish-based lunch sabotage, you'll cement your place as the office tosser everyone loves to hate.

So grab your notebook, start leveraging those synergies, and remember: when in doubt, just say, *"Let's circle back."* You're a fucking legend.

THE ART OF BEING AN EVERYDAY WANKER

Chapter Two

"How to Annoy Everyone Without Even Trying"

L ife isn't just a journey—it's a stage where your wankery can shine brightest. From mastering the group chat to being an insufferable coffee snob, this chapter will guide you through the small but significant ways you can irritate everyone around you.

1. The Group Chat Domination Technique

Group chats are a wanker's playground. They offer endless opportunities to derail conversations, avoid responsibility, and generally piss everyone off.

Wanker Tactics:

> **Derail with Nostalgia:** If someone asks, *"What time are we meeting?"* reply with, *"Haha, remember when Steve fell into the pond?"* The meeting time will never be decided, and everyone will hate you.
> **GIF Overload:** Spam random GIFs of Nicolas Cage or a dancing

baby. If someone asks you to stop, double down.
The Silent Spectator: Read every message but never reply. When called out, say, *"Just saw this now—sorry, been SO busy!"* (You weren't.)

> *Advanced Wanker Challenge: The WhatsApp Shenanigans*
> *Rename the group chat something absurd, like "The Council of Legends."*
> *Randomly leave the group, then ask to be re-added an hour later.*
> *Send a voice note for something that could have been a text. Bonus points if it's 5+ minutes long.*

2. Coffee Shop Shenanigans

Coffee shops are the sacred temples of everyday wankery, and your order is your scripture.

The Ultimate Wanker Order:

> *"Hi, I'll have a half-skim, half-oat caramel macchiato with a single shot of decaf espresso, extra foam, and a sprinkle of cinnamon. Oh, and make it extra hot."*
> If they get it wrong, sigh loudly and say, *"I guess this will do."*

Additional Moves:

Correct the barista's pronunciation of *"macchiato."* You're probably wrong, but do it with confidence.
Sit with your laptop open, pretending to work. Spend two hours scrolling Instagram while glaring at anyone looking for a table.

3. Social Media Bragging

Your Instagram, Twitter, and Facebook profiles are your platforms to showcase how much better your life is than everyone else's (even if it's not).

Wanker Post Types:

The Humblebrag: Post a photo of your new car with the caption: *"Hard work pays off #Blessed."*
The Inspirational Quote: Use a blurry sunset photo and add: *"The journey of a thousand miles begins with a single step."* You've just walked to the fridge for another beer.

The Vacation Flex:
Post photos of your feet by the pool. Caption: *"Work hard, play harder."* Everyone's rooting for the pool to swallow you whole.

Advanced Move:
Post a cryptic status like, *"Big things coming soon."* When people ask, refuse to elaborate. Nothing's coming.

Wanker Wisdom: Top Social Media Captions for Everyday Bragging
"Success is the best revenge." (Revenge on who? No one knows.)
"Some people dream of success. I make it happen." (You just cleaned the kitchen.)
"Currently manifesting greatness." (You're watching reruns of The Office.)

4. Pretending to Know About Wine

Being a wanker means confidently talking bollocks about things you know nothing about—wine being the ultimate example.

How to Fake It:

1. Swirl the glass aggressively, sniff it like you're a bloodhound on a case, and mutter, *"Ah, I'm getting hints of oak and blackcurrant."*
2. Say things like:
"It's bold, but with a soft finish."

"I really appreciate the tannins in this." (No one knows what tannins are.)

3. If someone challenges you, shrug and say, *"Wine is subjective."* This ends all arguments.

5. Grocery Store Power Moves

Even the mundane task of shopping can be an opportunity for everyday wankery.

Tips for Annoying Everyone in Tesco:

Walk slowly down the middle of the aisle, blocking everyone.
Ask an employee, *"Is this organic?"* about **everything**, including crisps.
Use the self-checkout, fail repeatedly, and loudly blame the machine. *"Unexpected item in the bagging area? Yeah, it's called my will to live."*

6. Gym Wanker Lite

Not ready for full gym wankery (see Chapter 10)? Start small.

Lightweight Moves:

Wear brand-new gym gear but do no actual exercise.
Spend 20 minutes stretching in front of the mirror, *"accidentally"* blocking someone's view.
Post a sweaty selfie after walking on the treadmill for three minutes. Caption: *"Back on the grind."*

Conclusion: The Glory of Everyday Wankery

Being an everyday wanker isn't about grand gestures; it's about the little things that make people quietly seethe while you sail through life unbothered. From group chats to coffee shops, you've got endless opportunities to annoy and delight in equal measure.

So grab your overpriced macchiato, post that humblebrag, and keep swirling your wine like you know what tannins are. You're not just an everyday wanker—you're the Picasso of petty chaos.

ROMANCE FOR WANKERS

Chapter Three

"Texts, Ghosts, and Questionable Tinder Photos"

L ove is a battlefield, and if you're reading this, you're probably one of the landmines. Romance as a wanker isn't about being smooth or charming; it's about leaning into your inherent twattery and hoping for the best. Whether you're single, dating, or three margaritas deep into a breakup spiral, this chapter will guide you through the minefield of modern love with all the grace of a drunk giraffe.

1. Texting Like a Tosser

The modern romance battlefield begins in the inbox. Crafting the perfect wanker text requires a mix of arrogance, ambiguity, and just enough effort to seem interesting without actually trying.

Rules for Texting Like a Pro Wanker:

Delay Tactics: Never reply immediately. Make them sweat. If they send *"Hey,"* wait 12 hours, then reply with, *"Hey, sorry, been so busy!"* You've been bingeing Love Island.
Emoji Overload: Use emojis to confuse, not clarify.
"Can't wait to see you later! *unicorn* *pizza* *bang* *octopus*"
If they question the octopus, they're clearly not your

soulmate.
Cryptic Messages: Leave them guessing with vague texts.
"Just saw a rainbow. Thought of you."
Thought of them how? Doesn't matter. Mystery is sexy.

Advanced Wanker Challenge: The 2 AM Text
Send: *"Hey, you up?"*
Follow up with: *"Never mind, wrong person."*
Congratulations, you've ruined their night and left them questioning their life choices.

2. Mastering the Art of Ghosting

Sometimes the best way to end things is to vanish like a fart in the wind. Ghosting is the sacred right of every wanker, but it requires finesse.

The Ghosting Playbook:

Phase Out Replies: Start responding with shorter and shorter texts.Them: *"How was your day?"*
You: *"Fine."*
Go Full Phantom: Stop replying altogether. Leave them staring at *"Delivered"* like a hopeful puppy.
The Resurrection Move: Pop back up three months later with, *"Hey, you crossed my mind today."* Translation: You're drunk and bored.

Warning: Ghosting is a double-edged sword. If done incorrectly, you might bump into them in Tesco. Have a fake apology ready: *"Sorry, I've just been **so** busy lately."*

3. The Tinder Tosser Toolkit

Your dating profile is your shop window, and you're selling yourself as the most eligible wanker around. The trick is to look like you tried *just enough*.

Profile Basics:

Bio: Keep it vague and self-important. *"6ft. Love adventures. Hate drama."*
Everyone loves adventures. No one knows what you mean by drama.

Photos:
A shirtless gym pic (even if you shouldn't).
A photo of you with a baby (not yours).
A blurry beach photo from 2014, showing you *"love to travel."*

The Opening Line: Start with something infuriatingly lazy, like *"Hey."* Or, if you're feeling bold, try, *"What's your star sign? I'm only compatible with Leos."*

Swipe Right on These Wanker Moves
Mention that you *"love the gym"* but never elaborate.
Brag about your pasta-making skills. Everyone loves carbs.
Use a dog in your profile photo, even if it's not your dog. Especially if it's not your dog.

Swipe Right on These Wanker Moves
Mention that you "love the gym" but never elaborate.
Brag about your pasta-making skills. Everyone loves carbs.
Use a dog in your profile photo, even if it's not your dog. Especially if it's not your dog.

4. The Relationship Wanker

Once you've hoodwinked someone into a relationship, it's time to keep things interesting (for you, at least).

Wanker Habits in a Relationship:

Argue About Pointless Shit: Pineapple on pizza? Whether it's called a duvet or a quilt? Stir the pot and enjoy the chaos.
The Instagram Couple: Post a photo of your partner with the caption:
"When you know, you know."
You've been dating for three weeks.
Petty Revenge: If they piss you off, put the toilet roll on backwards. They'll never notice, but you'll feel victorious.

5. Breakup Shenanigans

Every wanker knows that breakups aren't the end—they're the beginning of a drama-filled new chapter.

The Post-Breakup Playbook:

The Cryptic Status Update: Post something like:
"Sometimes, you just have to let go to grow."
Everyone will know you've been dumped.
Revenge Glow-Up: Join a gym, get a haircut, and post selfies captioned: *"Feeling myself."* You're still crying in the shower.
Accidental Encounters: *"Bump into them"* at their favourite coffee shop. Act shocked: *"Oh, I didn't know you came here!"* You did.

Conclusion: Love Like a Wanker

Romance isn't about being perfect—it's about being memorable. Whether you're sending cryptic texts, ghosting your way to freedom, or ruining their night with a 2 a.m. message, remember: love is messy, ridiculous, and often infuriating.

But as long as you're the wanker in control of the chaos, you're doing it right. Now go forth, swipe boldly, and remember—if all else fails, there's always wine.

WANKER ON THE TOWN

Chapter Four

"How to Be the Absolute Worst (and Love It)"

G oing out isn't just a night of fun—it's a stage where your wankery can truly shine. Whether you're dominating the pub, commandeering a club, or causing chaos in a late-night kebab shop, this chapter will teach you how to leave a trail of irritation and awkward laughter wherever you go.

Pub Shenanigans

The pub is a wanker's natural habitat—a place where pint glasses are full, egos are high, and opportunities to piss people off are endless.

Tips for Being a Pub Wanker:

The Overconfident Orderer: Spend ten minutes asking the bartender about craft beers. After extensive deliberation, order a Guinness and then complain loudly that it's *"not poured properly."*

Table Tyranny: Claim the biggest table with your coat and bag, even if you're alone. Refuse to move, even when a group of eight clearly needs it.

Toasting Twattery: Randomly shout *"TO THE LADS!"* or

"CHEERS TO SUCCESS!" at intervals, regardless of whether anyone joins in. You're drinking alone, but that's irrelevant.

Advanced Move:
Start a singalong to a song that isn't playing. Bonus points if it's *Wonderwall*. Extra bonus points if people actually join in.

> *The Wanker's Pub Quiz Survival Guide*
> ***Team Name:*** *Choose something obnoxious like "Let's Get Quizzical" or "Quiz Me Baby One More Time."*
> ***Answer Strategy:*** *Shout, "It's definitely D!" for every question, even if the answers are numbers.*
> ***Tiebreaker Drama:*** *Argue with the quizmaster over the correct spelling of "moussaka." Be wrong. Double down anyway.*

2. Clubbing Catastrophes

Clubs are where wankers can unleash their full chaotic energy. This is your time to shine—or at least blind everyone with your terrible dance moves.

Dance Floor Moves:

> **The Air DJ:** Stand in the middle of the dance floor, waving your arms like you're mixing tracks. You're not.
> **The Circle Starter:** Try to form a dance circle. Nobody joins. You keep trying.
> **The Invisible Mic:** Sing loudly and off-key to a song you don't know the words to. Bonus points for pointing at strangers like they're backup singers.

The Bar Strategy:

Order the most complicated cocktail on the menu during peak hours. Complain when it takes too long.
Chat up the bartender with lines like, *"So, how long have you been…*

bartending?" They hate you.

Clubbing Wanker Pro-Tips
Wear sunglasses. Indoors. At night.
Carry a vape pen that lights up. Blow smoke rings in people's faces.
Take 15 selfies in the bathroom. Caption one, "Absolute scenes tonight."

3. The Late-Night Kebab Shop Showdown

The night isn't complete until you've made a scene in the kebab shop.

Power Moves:

The Over-Orderer: Ask for a kebab with *"everything on it."* When it arrives, say, *"I didn't mean onions."*
Pavement Picnic: Drop half your chips on the floor. Pick them up. Eat them anyway.
Reflection Rant: Argue with your reflection in the shop window. *"What are you looking at, mate?"* Everyone watching agrees with your reflection.

Advanced Move:
Pretend to be the chef. Lean over the counter and critique their garlic sauce.

4. Taxi Tossery

Getting home is an opportunity for one last act of wankery.

In the Taxi:

Backseat DJ: Insist on controlling the music. Play *Mr. Brightside* on repeat.

Unnecessary Directions: Give detailed instructions for a route the driver already knows. *"Mate, I think you need to turn left here. No, the other left."*

The Escape Artist: Claim you have *"cash at home"* and bolt out of the cab before paying.

Advanced Move:

Fall asleep halfway through the journey, wake up confused, and yell, *"This isn't my house!"* It is.

Conclusion: Wanker in the Wild

Being a wanker on the town isn't just about having a good time —it's about making sure everyone around you remembers your presence, whether they want to or not. From the pub to the club to the kebab shop, your mission is simple: dominate the night with arrogance, chaos, and just enough charm to keep from being thrown out.

So go forth, pint in hand, and remember: if you're not annoying at least one person by the end of the night, are you even trying?

WANKER WISDOM

Chapter Five

*"Unsolicited Advice for a Life
of Glorious Cockery"*

Some people seek wisdom from ancient philosophers or self-help gurus. Others turn to Sir Knobulous W. Pompington, a man who once said, *"The only thing better than being right is making everyone else feel wrong."* This chapter is your crash course in delivering life advice that nobody asked for, applying questionable logic to everyday situations, and offering pearls of wisdom polished in the dirt of pure wankery.

1. The Wanker's Guide to Deep-Sounding Nonsense

The art of wanker wisdom isn't about actually being wise—it's about sounding wise while saying absolutely nothing.

Tips for Delivering Fake Profundity:

Use vague phrases that sound important:
"Sometimes, you have to lose yourself to truly find yourself."
(Translation: You got lost in Ikea again.)

Turn everyday experiences into metaphors:
"This coffee is like life—bittersweet and overpriced."

Add dramatic pauses. For example:
"You know... life isn't about waiting for the storm to pass... it's

about learning to dance in the rain." (Cue eye rolls.)
Advanced Move:
Misquote famous people for extra flair:
"As Gandhi said, 'Treat yourself.'"

2. Offer Useless Advice at Every Opportunity

Wankers excel at dispensing unsolicited wisdom, often when it's least needed or least appropriate.

Classic Wanker Advice Moves:

To someone stressed: *"Just relax."* Groundbreaking.
To someone single: *"You'll find love when you stop looking."* Thanks, Socrates.
To someone broke: *"Maybe stop buying lattes."* Revolutionary financial advice.

Advanced Move:
Give advice on topics you know nothing about.
"Oh, you're building a deck? You should really look into sustainable wood options."
(You don't know the difference between plywood and particleboard.)

Wankerisms for Everyday Life
"The journey is the reward." (You're lost.)
"Everything happens for a reason." (It doesn't.)
"Failing to plan is planning to fail." (You just forgot to buy milk.)

3. Live Like You're the Main Character

The secret to wanker-level wisdom is behaving as though your life is a movie, and everyone else is just a supporting character.

Main Character Energy Tips:

Dramatic Train Staring: Sit by the window, gaze into the distance, and think deep thoughts while listening to sad music. Bonus points if it's raining.
Big Gestures: Make mountains out of molehills. For example:
"I had to walk TWO extra blocks because Starbucks was out of oat milk. Life's so hard right now."
Overanalyse Everything: If someone texts, "K," assume they hate you. Start a full existential crisis.

Advanced Move:
Narrate your own life in your head.
"She stepped into the meeting room, coffee in hand, fully aware that today, she would dominate."
(You're about to give a PowerPoint presentation on printer usage.)

❖ ❖ ❖

4. Misuse Big Words to Sound Smarter

Wankers love dropping fancy words into everyday conversation, even if they don't fully understand them.

Wanker Vocabulary 101:

Juxtaposition: Use it to describe anything remotely contrasting.
"The juxtaposition of this burger with fries is genius."
Existential: Toss it into casual chats about your weekend.
"Brunch was an existential experience."
Paradigm: No one knows what it means, so just go for it.
"We're really shifting paradigms here."
Advanced Move:
Use Latin phrases to intimidate people.
"Per se, this isn't prima facie *a good idea, but* carpe diem, *right?"*

❖ ❖ ❖

5. Take Credit for Everything

Wankers are experts at making themselves look good, even when they've done absolutely nothing.

How to Claim Credit:

The "We" Move: When someone else does the work, say, *"I think we really nailed that project."*
The Retrospective Genius: If an idea turns out to be good, claim it was yours. If it flops, say you *"had concerns from the start."*
The Bold Bluff: When someone explains something, nod and say, *"That's exactly what I was thinking."* It wasn't.

❖ ❖ ❖

> *Advanced Wanker Challenge: Make Everything About You*
> Friend: "I just got a promotion!"
> You: "Oh, I know how that feels. When I got mine, it was so overwhelming."
> Friend: "I'm getting married!"
> You: "Weddings are so stressful. Let me tell you about mine…"
> Friend: "I just lost my dog."
> You: "Yeah, I had a goldfish once. So hard."

❖ ❖ ❖

6. Overanalyse Everything Like a Philosopher

When in doubt, blow a minor event out of proportion and make it sound like a revelation.

Examples of Overanalysing Like a Wanker:

> "Why do we even call it 'rush hour' if nothing's moving? It's a metaphor for life, isn't it?"
> "When you think about it, sandwiches are just edible containers for feelings."
> "What if WiFi signals are actually controlling our thoughts?"

Advanced Move:
Start a conspiracy theory. Make it so ridiculous that people actually consider it.
"Big Salad doesn't want us to know the truth about croutons."

❖ ❖ ❖

Conclusion: Be the Philosopher Nobody Asked For

Being a wanker isn't about actually solving problems—it's about making everyone believe you know what you're talking about, even when you clearly don't. From delivering unsolicited advice to overanalysing the meaning of brunch, wanker wisdom is all about turning the mundane into the profound (and occasionally infuriating).

So go forth, my philosophical arseholes. Offer advice nobody wants, sprinkle big words into conversations, and live like you're the main character in a poorly written soap opera. Remember: if people aren't rolling their eyes at you, you're not doing it right.

❖ ❖ ❖

WANKERS UNITE

Chapter Six

"Finding Your Tribe of Tosspots"

◆ ◆ ◆

No wanker is an island. Sure, you can dominate group chats, ruin nights out, and hog office glory all on your own, but the true joy of wankery lies in finding like-minded tosspots to share the chaos with. This chapter is your guide to building a community of glorious arseholes, bonding over mutual pettiness, and wreaking havoc as a united front.

◆ ◆ ◆

1. How to Spot a Fellow Wanker

Wankers are everywhere—your coworkers, your gym buddies, even your second cousin who keeps telling you about their *"personal brand."* Spotting them requires a keen eye for arrogance, chaos, and overly curated Instagram posts.

Signs You've Found a Kindred Wanker:

They wear sunglasses indoors and insist it's for *"the vibe."*
They unironically say things like, *"I'm just so* me *right now."*
They correct your pronunciation of *"quinoa"* without knowing if they're right.
They turn every group outing into a photo op, complete with hashtags like #SquadGoals.

Advanced Move:
Test them with a subtle wanker challenge. Say, *"Pineapple on pizza is an abomination,"* and see if they passionately agree or argue. Either response confirms their status.

♦ ♦ ♦

2. Building Your Tribe

Once you've identified your fellow tossers, it's time to bond over shared pettiness and mutual love for stirring the pot.

Wanker Icebreakers:

Start a debate over the most pointless topic imaginable: *"Is water technically wet?"*
Share your most obnoxious humblebrag: *"I'm so tired from my yoga retreat in Bali. Life's just so* full *right now."*
Play a round of *"Who's the Biggest Knob?"* (Spoiler: It's all of you.)

♦ ♦ ♦

> *Wanker Pro-Tip: Host a Gathering of Tosspots*
> *Theme: "Overdressed for No Reason."*
> *Dress Code: Formalwear with Crocs.*
> *Activity: Argue about the correct way to pronounce "scone" until someone cries.*
> *Party Favour: Tiny bottles of artisanal gin no one asked for.*

♦ ♦ ♦

3. Group Activities for Wankers

Once your tribe is established, it's time to create memories of mutual annoyance.
Activity Ideas:

The Brunch Debacle: Take over a café and spend 45 minutes debating whether avocado toast is *actually* worth £12.

The Pub Quiz Takeover: Argue every answer, insist the quizmaster is biased, and lose spectacularly.

The Museum "Experts": Walk through an art exhibit loudly misinterpreting every piece. *"This sculpture obviously represents the futility of modern relationships."* It's a fire extinguisher.

Advanced Move:

Start an impromptu debate about the deeper meaning of the fire extinguisher. Leave only when escorted out.

◆ ◆ ◆

4. Wanker Wars: The Downside of the Tribe

As glorious as it is to gather a group of tosspots, things can go sideways. When you put too much chaos in one room, egos collide.

Common Wanker Conflicts:

The Instagram Fight: One wanker posts the group photo with a filter that makes everyone else look terrible. Prepare for passive-aggressive comments.

The Foodie Feud: Someone critiques the chef's plating at a restaurant. *"Honestly, the microgreens are so 2020."* Fisticuffs ensue.

The Buzzword Battle: At some point, two wankers will compete over who can use the most corporate jargon in a single sentence. *"I think we need to leverage our synergy to ideate scalable solutions."*

Resolution Strategy:

Settle disputes with a drinking game. Loser has to apologise sincerely—a fate worse than death for any wanker.

◆ ◆ ◆

5. Creating a Legacy of Chaos

True wanker tribes don't just live for the moment; they aim to leave an impression—preferably a mildly irritating one.

Ways to Cement Your Legacy:

Start a group hashtag and use it relentlessly: #WankerSquad.
Hold an annual *"Wanker Olympics"* with events like:
   The Passive-Aggressive Email Sprint.
   The Instagram Caption-Off.
   Buzzword Bingo.
Make a pact to always defend each other in online comment sections, no matter how wrong or ridiculous the argument.

◆ ◆ ◆

The Official Wanker Squad Commandments
Thou shalt always be overdressed.
Thou shalt never admit fault.
Thou shalt correct others, even when thou art wrong.
Thou shalt take selfies in every reflective surface.
Thou shalt leave no brunch unfinished.

◆ ◆ ◆

Conclusion: Strength in Tossery

The beauty of being a wanker isn't just in your ability to annoy —it's in sharing that talent with others. A great wanker tribe amplifies your chaos, supports your nonsense, and ensures that no social event is ever dull again. Together, you're unstoppable.

So gather your fellow tosspots, start planning your Wanker Olympics, and remember: the more people you irritate, the stronger your bond becomes.

◆ ◆ ◆

WANKER AT HOME

Chapter Seven

"How to Annoy Everyone Without Leaving Your Sofa"

◆ ◆ ◆

Home may be where the heart is, but it's also where your wankery can truly thrive. From commandeering the TV remote to ruining shared living spaces with your unapologetic laziness, this chapter is your ultimate guide to being a top-tier tosser in your own castle.

◆ ◆ ◆

1. The Netflix Dictator

Streaming services are the modern battlefield of domestic life, and you are the tyrant ruling over the remote with an iron fist.

How to Assert Your Authority:

Scroll Domination: Spend 15 minutes endlessly scrolling through options, then decide to rewatch *The Office* for the 12th time.
Genre Wars: If someone suggests a genre, immediately dismiss it.
"A rom-com? Ew, we're watching true crime. It's educational."
Passive Aggressive Power Play: Ask, "What do you want to watch?" and then pick something completely different.

Advanced Move:
Pretend to be magnanimous by saying, *"Fine, you can pick,"* then complain loudly throughout their choice. *"Ugh, this plot makes no sense."*

◆ ◆ ◆

Wanker Pro-Tip: The 'Just One More' Trick
Convince everyone to stay up for "just one more episode." Repeat until it's 3 a.m. Then say, "Wow, you guys have no self-control."

◆ ◆ ◆

2. Cooking Shenanigans

The kitchen is your playground, and every meal is an opportunity to show off your wankery while annoying everyone else in the house.

Culinary Wanker Moves:

   Overcomplicate Everything: Make *"artisan"* toast by slightly tilting the bread on the plate. Add a drizzle of balsamic glaze and declare it *"elevated."*
   Instagram the Evidence: Take 15 photos of your meal before eating. Post it with hashtags like #FoodPorn and #ChefLife.
   Leave a Trail of Chaos: Use every pot and pan in the kitchen for a single omelette. Refuse to do the washing up.

Advanced Move:
Critique everyone else's food like you're a Michelin inspector. *"The flavours are... okay, but it's a bit one-note."*

◆ ◆ ◆

3. DIY Disasters

Home improvement is a chance to flex your creativity—and your utter incompetence.

How to Fail Spectacularly:

The Over-planner: Spend three days watching YouTube tutorials, then abandon the project halfway through.
The Miscalculation Master: Build a bookshelf that's slightly tilted and say it's *"modern design."*
The Tools Dictator: Borrow everyone's tools but never return them. If asked, say, *"It's somewhere in the garage."* You don't have a garage.

❖ ❖ ❖

> *The Wanker's DIY Commandments*
> *Thou shalt always make a bigger mess than the original problem.*
> *Thou shalt insist it's "a work in progress" indefinitely.*
> *Thou shalt never read the instructions.*

❖ ❖ ❖

4. Domestic Laziness with Style

Even your laziness can be an art form when done correctly.

Techniques for Maximum Annoyance:

The Empty Carton Gambit: Leave an empty milk carton in the fridge and say, *"I thought someone might want to recycle it."*
The Laundry Loophole: Dump clean laundry on the sofa and insist it's *"just airing out."* Never fold it.
The Strategic Nap: Fall asleep on the couch during household chores, then wake up and say, *"Oh, sorry, I didn't know we were cleaning."*

Advanced Move:
Claim the TV remote while *"napping."* Refuse to let anyone change the channel.

❖ ❖ ❖

5. The Shared Bathroom Saboteur

Bathrooms are sacred spaces—perfect for pushing boundaries and creating chaos.

How to Annoy Everyone:

Leave hair everywhere: in the sink, the shower, and somehow on the ceiling.
Use the last of the toilet roll and leave the empty tube on the holder. When confronted, say, *"I was saving it for you."*
Take 45-minute showers and act surprised when someone else needs hot water.

Advanced Move:
Borrow someone else's fancy shampoo and fill the bottle with water when it runs out.

❖ ❖ ❖

6. Hosting as a Wanker

Having guests over is a prime opportunity to show off your most irritating habits.

Hosting Wanker Moves:

Serve drinks in mismatched glasses and call it *"quirky."*
Talk endlessly about your *"signature dish,"* then serve burnt pasta.
Insist everyone take their shoes off at the door, even though your floor is covered in crumbs and dog hair.

❖ ❖ ❖

Advanced Wanker Challenge: The Guest-room Chaos
Provide a pillow with barely any stuffing.
Forget to change the sheets and say, "They're vintage."
Serve breakfast at 11:45 a.m. and call it brunch.

❖ ❖ ❖

Conclusion: Reigning as the Wanker of Your Castle

Home is where you can truly embrace your inner wanker without judgment (well, minimal judgment). Whether you're bossing the TV, failing at DIY, or hosting guests with unmatched chaos, the goal is simple: make every moment slightly more inconvenient for those around you.

So put your feet up on the coffee table, grab the remote, and bask in the glory of being the undisputed tosser of your domain. Remember, it's not laziness—it's lifestyle curation.

❖ ❖ ❖

THE EXISTENTIAL WANKER

Chapter Eight

"Why Are We Here (and Why Does It Matter?)"

Every wanker eventually faces The Big Questions: What is the meaning of life? Why does my cat hate me? What happens to lost socks? These late-night existential crises are a rite of passage for tossers everywhere. This chapter is your guide to embracing those moments of profound overthinking with the confidence and chaos only a true wanker can muster.

◆ ◆ ◆

1. The 2 A.M. Existential Crisis

The best time to question your entire existence is when you should be sleeping. This is when your brain decides to dig up embarrassing memories from 2008 and ponder the mysteries of the universe.

Common 2 A.M. Thoughts of a Wanker:

> "Why do we call it a building if it's already built?"
> "Do I even like my job, or am I just faking it?" (Spoiler: you're definitely faking it.)

"What if we're all just characters in someone else's poorly written fan-fiction?"

How to Handle It:

Google pointless questions like, *"How many ants would it take to lift a car?"*

Post a cryptic status update:
   "Feeling lost. Don't DM."

Try to sleep, fail, and end up buying unnecessary crap online.

Advanced Move:

Start journaling your thoughts, but only write one entry titled *"Life is Weird"* before abandoning the notebook forever.

◆ ◆ ◆

> **Wanker Pro-Tip: The Existential Shopping Spree**
> *Nothing soothes an existential crisis like retail therapy. Buy things that scream "I'm deep," such as:*
>   *A vintage globe you'll never use.*
>   *A journal titled Manifest Your Dreams.*
>   *A poster of Albert Einstein with the quote, "Imagination is more important than knowledge."*

◆ ◆ ◆

2. Spiritual Wankery

When grappling with The Big Questions, many wankers turn to spirituality. Not in the traditional sense, of course—wankers prefer vague, Instagrammable enlightenment.

Signs You've Entered the Spiritual Wanker Phase:

You buy crystals and assign them arbitrary powers. *"This one wards off bad vibes."*

You start saying, *"I'm really into energy work,"* but can't explain what that means.

You burn sage, claim it's for *"negative energy,"* and then set off the fire alarm.

Advanced Move:
Go to one yoga class and immediately declare yourself *"spiritually enlightened."* Start dropping words like *"chakra"* and *"namaste"* into casual conversations.

❖ ❖ ❖

3. Fake Deep Activities

Being an existential wanker means leaning into activities that make you feel profound—even if they're completely ridiculous.

Recommended Activities:

Lie on the floor and stare at the ceiling. Tell anyone who asks that you're *"centering your energy."*
Visit an art gallery and loudly misinterpret every piece.
   "This blank canvas represents the void we all feel inside."
   It's just a blank canvas.
Spend an afternoon in a park, journal in hand, pretending to write poetry. Actually, you're just doodling flowers.

Advanced Move:
Start a podcast called *Life, the Universe, and Bollocks*. Record one episode and quit.

❖ ❖ ❖

Wanker Wisdom: Deep Questions to Ponder
"If we're all unique, doesn't that make us the same?"
"Is cereal a soup?"
"Why is abbreviation such a long word?"

❖ ❖ ❖

4. Conspiracy Theories for the Aspiring Wanker

True wankers know that questioning everything includes dabbling in wild conspiracy theories.

Popular Conspiracies for Wankers:

"The moon landing was staged. You can tell because the shadows are too shadowy."
"WiFi signals are actually controlling our thoughts."
"Big Salad doesn't want us to know the truth about croutons."

Advanced Move:
Create your own ridiculous theory and convince others to believe it. For example:
"Birds aren't real. They're government drones recharging on power lines."

◆ ◆ ◆

5. Turning Overthinking into a Superpower

Overthinking is the wanker's secret weapon. Why solve a problem when you can spend hours dissecting it until it's ten times worse?

Overthinking Techniques:

Rehearse conversations you've already had, thinking of better comebacks.
Spend 45 minutes debating whether you should send a text, then send "K."
Ponder life's unanswerable questions, like:
  "Did I peak in high school?"
  (You didn't, but it's fun to think about.)

Advanced Move:
Overthink something so much that you convince yourself it doesn't matter anymore. *"Is this important? No, wait—it's fine. Or is it?"*

◆ ◆ ◆

6. Finding Meaning in Meaninglessness

When you've exhausted all other avenues, it's time to embrace the absurdity of existence.

How to Make Peace with Life's Chaos:

> Laugh at the fact that you're crying over burnt toast.
> Celebrate small victories, like remembering where you parked your car.
> Accept that sometimes, the only answer to life's big questions is: *Fuck it.*

Advanced Move:
Throw a party celebrating life's randomness. Serve toast with no toppings, call it *"minimalist cuisine,"* and toast to *"the universe's magnificent chaos."*

❖ ❖ ❖

Conclusion: Leaning Into the Void

Life doesn't come with a manual, but if it did, you'd probably lose it under the sofa. The secret to being an existential wanker is embracing the chaos, overthinking everything, and finding joy in asking questions you'll never answer.

So grab your crystals, burn some sage (responsibly this time), and remember: life is weird, you're weird, and that's exactly how it's meant to be.

❖ ❖ ❖

WANKERS OF THE WORLD

Chapter Nine

"How to Be a Pain in the Arse While Traveling"

❖ ❖ ❖

Travel is the perfect opportunity to take your wankery on tour. Whether you're annoying fellow passengers on a plane, dominating the local pub quiz in a foreign country, or mispronouncing menu items with confidence, this chapter will teach you how to leave a trail of chaos, confusion, and eye rolls across the globe.

❖ ❖ ❖

1. Aeroplane Antics

Planes are a microcosm of human suffering—cramped seats, questionable food, and crying babies. It's your duty as a wanker to make it worse.

Classic Moves:

The Armrest Tyrant: Claim both armrests and then sigh loudly when your seat-mate dares to reclaim one.
Recliner Rebel: Slam your seat back the moment the seatbelt sign turns off, even if the person behind you is 6'5" and clearly

suffering.

Carry-On Chaos: Bring an oversized bag and stuff it into the overhead compartment like you're playing Tetris. Bonus points if you have to unpack half of it in the aisle.

Advanced Move:

Clap when the plane lands. If nobody joins in, clap louder and shout, *"Great job, team!"*

❖ ❖ ❖

> **Wanker Pro-Tip: The In-Flight Experience**
> Take your shoes off immediately. Bonus points for wearing socks with holes.
> Complain loudly about turbulence as though it's a personal attack.
> Order tomato juice and explain that it "just tastes better at altitude."

❖ ❖ ❖

2. Tourist Tossery

When traveling, you're not just a visitor—you're an ambassador of wankery. Your mission: to dominate every landmark, attraction, and café with your unparalleled ability to annoy.

The Golden Rules of Tourism Wankery:

The Photo Hog: Take 47 photos of the same landmark from slightly different angles. Post every single one with captions like, *"Stunning," "Speechless,"* and *"Take me back already."*

The Culture Clanger: Loudly mispronounce local words while insisting you're "trying to be authentic."

   "Bonjourno! Gracias, amigo!" (You're in Paris.)

The Foodie Fraud: Order the most exotic dish on the menu, take one bite, and say, *"Mmm, interesting."* Then leave the rest untouched.

Advanced Move:

Buy a tacky souvenir (like a snow globe or fridge magnet) and declare it *"a piece of local art."*

❖ ❖ ❖

> **The Wanker's Packing List**
> A portable speaker to blast your playlist at inappropriate times.
> A giant hat that obstructs everyone else's view.
> A guidebook that you'll never actually read but will hold for Instagram photos.

❖ ❖ ❖

3. The Hotel Hijinks

Hotels are where wankers thrive. Between unnecessary complaints and questionable behaviour, you can make your presence unforgettable.

Hotel Wanker Moves:

> **The Upgrade Whisperer:** Complain that your room *"doesn't match the pictures online."* Hint that you're an influencer.
> **Breakfast Buffet Bandit:** Pile your plate with food you'll never eat. Wrap a croissant in a napkin *"for later."*
> **Poolside Drama:** *"Reserve"* a sun lounger with your towel at 6 a.m., then disappear for half the day.

Advanced Move:
Call the front desk at midnight to ask how to turn on the shower.

❖ ❖ ❖

4. Public Transport Pest

Public transport is a shared experience, but you're here to make it all about you.

How to Be the Worst on Trains, Buses, and Beyond:

> Play music out loud instead of using headphones. Bonus

points for a questionable playlist.
Take up two seats with your bag. When asked to move it, act deeply offended.
Have a loud phone conversation about something nobody wants to hear:

"*Yeah, mate, the rash is still there. Doctor says it might be fungal.*"

❖ ❖ ❖

Advanced Wanker Challenge: Public Transport Edition
Stand in the aisle when there are empty seats.
Announce every stop like you're the conductor.
Eat something smelly, like boiled eggs or tuna sandwiches.

❖ ❖ ❖

5. Souvenirs Nobody Wants

A true wanker knows that no trip is complete without bringing home pointless crap to clutter someone else's life.

The Ultimate Wanker Souvenirs:

Tacky T-shirts with slogans like, "I '*heart*' [Insert City]."
Magnets, snow globes, or shot glasses—because nothing says cultural appreciation like mass-produced junk.
A giant straw hat or poncho that you'll never wear again but insist was "*a vibe.*"

Advanced Move:
Gift a friend an unidentifiable local delicacy. "*It's pickled something—I thought you'd love it.*"

❖ ❖ ❖

6. The Return Home: Bragging Rights

Once the trip is over, your next job is to milk it for all it's worth.

Post-Trip Bragging:
Post every photo on social media with captions like, *"This place changed me."*
Start every conversation with, *"When I was in [Destination]…"* even if it's irrelevant.
Critique your local coffee shop by saying, *"It's good, but it's nothing like the espresso in Florence."*

Advanced Move:
Casually mention your trip in a way that derails someone else's story.
   Them: *"I had the best pizza last night."*
   You: *"Oh, you simply* must *try pizza in 'Napoli'. Everything else is just bread with toppings."*

◆ ◆ ◆

Conclusion: Globetrotting Wanker Extraordinaire

Traveling as a wanker isn't just about seeing the world—it's about leaving your mark on it (preferably in the form of mild annoyance and unforgettable photo captions). From airports to landmarks to public transport, your mission is clear: be unapologetically you, wherever you go.

So pack your oversized hat, brush up on your mispronunciations, and prepare to conquer the world, one eye roll at a time.

◆ ◆ ◆

WANKER FITNESS

Chapter Ten

"How to Be the Worst Person at the Gym"

Gyms are more than just places to get fit—they're arenas of competition, performance, and public judgment. As a wanker, your mission is clear: dominate the gym floor with the kind of confidence that screams, "I don't need results; I just need attention." This chapter will guide you through the art of gym wankery, from over-the-top selfies to inappropriate grunting.

◆ ◆ ◆

1. The Instagram Athlete

No gym session is complete without broadcasting your "effort" to your followers. After all, if it's not on Instagram, did it even happen?

How to Nail the Gym Selfie:

    Timing Is Everything: Take the photo before you've broken a sweat. Nobody wants to see your red face and uneven sweat patches.
    Pose Like a Pro: Flex aggressively in front of the mirror while pretending to look casual. Bonus points for angling your phone just right to show off your *"progress."*
    The Caption Game: Use hashtags like #NoPainNoGain,

#FitFam, and #BeastMode even if you've only walked on the treadmill.

Advanced Move:
Post a video of yourself lifting an embarrassingly light weight but slap on motivational music to make it look epic.

❖ ❖ ❖

> *Wanker Pro-Tip: The Ultimate Gym Caption*
> "Early bird catches the worm, but this beast catches gains. #GrindNeverStops"

❖ ❖ ❖

2. Equipment Hogging 101

The gym has limited machines, but that doesn't mean you need to share.

Hogging Strategies:

The Triple Threat: Use three machines at once for your *"circuit training."* Guilt-trip anyone who asks if you're done.
The Timer Dodger: Sit on a machine scrolling Instagram between sets. If someone asks how many sets you have left, reply, *"Oh, I'm just getting started."*
The Towel Claim: Drape your towel over equipment you're thinking about using. Leave it there indefinitely.

Advanced Move:
When someone asks to work in with you, act offended. *"Um, I'm kind of in the zone right now."*

❖ ❖ ❖

3. Grunting and Groaning Like a Pro

Making noise is a key part of gym wankery. The louder you are, the more people will notice you (and wish you weren't there).

How to Perfect Your Grunt:

Start small with a low *"huh"* on light weights.
Build up to a full-on *"AAAAARGH!"* during your heaviest lifts (which might still be lighter than everyone else's warm-up).
End with a triumphant drop of the weights, ensuring they make maximum noise.

Advanced Move:
Yell, *"LET'S GO!"* before every set. Say it again afterward for no reason.

❖ ❖ ❖

Wanker's Noise Chart
Light Grunt: "Huh!" (Annoying, but tolerable.)
Mid-Level Groan: "UGH!" (People are staring.)
Full Scream: "YAAARGH!" (Everyone is leaving.)

❖ ❖ ❖

4. Gym Wardrobe Malfunctions (On Purpose)

Your outfit says a lot about you, and as a gym wanker, it should scream *"LOOK AT ME!"*

What to Wear:

The Tank Top Too Soon: Wear a tank top even if your arms look more like spaghetti than rigatoni.
The Leggings Lad: Compression leggings with nothing over them. It's a statement, but nobody knows what you're saying.
The Branded Bragger: Deck yourself out in the most expensive activewear you can find. Bonus points for matching water bottles and towels.

Advanced Move:
Wear a weightlifting belt for every exercise—even if you're just

doing bicep curls.

❖ ❖ ❖

5. The "Trainer" Without Credentials

You don't need a certification to give unsolicited fitness advice—just confidence and a loud voice.

How to Be the Worst Fake Trainer:

> Offer tips to strangers, even when they didn't ask. *"You're squatting all wrong, mate. Let me show you."*
> Correct someone's form while they're mid-set, ensuring maximum annoyance.
> Use phrases like, *"I read somewhere that..."* to justify your nonsense.

Advanced Move:
Carry a clipboard to look official. Take notes on people's form as if you're scouting talent.

❖ ❖ ❖

6. Yoga Class Shenanigans

Yoga is meant to be a calming, meditative experience—but not when you're there.

Yoga Wanker Moves:

> Arrive late and unroll your mat dramatically, knocking over someone else's water bottle.
> Giggle during downward dog and whisper, *"This one's so awkward!"*
> End the session with an overly dramatic *"NAMASTE,"* bowing to everyone like you're a spiritual guru.

Advanced Move:

Use a giant, fluorescent yoga mat that takes up twice the space of a normal one.

◆ ◆ ◆

7. Post-Gym Wanker Rituals
The workout isn't over until you've made sure everyone knows you've been to the gym.

Post-Workout Behaviour:

> Walk into the locker room and loudly announce, *"What a session!"*
> Spend 15 minutes flexing in the mirror while pretending to towel off.
> Drink a protein shake so aggressively that you spill half of it. Say, *"It's all part of the grind."*

Advanced Move:
Leave sweaty handprints on every surface as a *"badge of honour."*

◆ ◆ ◆

Conclusion: Flex, Sweat, Repeat

The gym isn't just a place to exercise—it's a stage for your wankery to truly shine. From hogging equipment to grunting like a maniac, the goal is to make sure everyone knows you're there, whether they like it or not.

So grab your towel, crank up the noise, and remember: it's not about results; it's about the performance. Flex hard, wank harder.

◆ ◆ ◆

WANKER PARENTING

Chapter Eleven

"How to Raise Mini-Wankers"

❖ ❖ ❖

Parenting is one of life's greatest challenges—and for a wanker, it's also one of life's greatest opportunities. This is your chance to pass on your unique brand of chaos to the next generation, raising tiny versions of yourself to annoy the world long after you're gone. Whether you're a parent, godparent, or just the *"fun uncle/aunt,"* this chapter will teach you how to nurture pint-sized tosspots with pride.

❖ ❖ ❖

1. Overachieving Parents

The key to being a wanker parent is making every mundane milestone feel like the discovery of fire.

How to Overdo It:

- Post every achievement on social media:
  "Little Freddie tied his shoes today! So proud! #Blessed #ShoelaceGoals"
  (Don't mention he's 14.)
- Enrol your child in absurd activities to one-up other parents:
  "Oh, Jessica's doing baby Pilates. It's so important to build core strength early."
- Argue with other parents about whose kid is more "gifted."

Use phrases like, *"He's just very advanced for his age,"* even if he's just eating crayons faster than the others.

Advanced Move:
Claim your child is fluent in French after they master *bonjour* and *croissant*.

◆ ◆ ◆

Wanker Pro-Tip: The Perfect School Drop-Off
Wear athleisure to suggest you're heading to yoga (you're not).
Blast classical music loudly as you pull up.
Shout, "Be brilliant!" as your kid gets out, ensuring everyone hears.

◆ ◆ ◆

2. Raising Drama Kings and Queens

Encourage your child's natural flair for theatrics. After all, the world's a stage, and your little tosser is the star.

Tips for Cultivating Chaos:

Teach them the fine art of exaggeration.
   "You didn't get dessert" = child abuse.
Encourage public tantrums: *"It's just how they express themselves."*
Reward petty behaviour with treats. If they snitch on their sibling, give them an extra biscuit. Life's a competition.

Advanced Move:
Stage *"family debates"* over minor issues like which crayon colour is best. Treat them like UN negotiations.

◆ ◆ ◆

3. The School Wanker

School is a goldmine of opportunities to flex your parenting wankery.

How to Dominate the PTA:

Demand gluten-free, sugar-free, cruelty-free biscuits at every event—even if nobody asked.

Use your child's science project to show off your *"creativity."*
  "Oh, we built a fully functional volcano that also teaches kids about recycling!" (You did it; the kid just watched.)

Correct other parents' grammar in PTA WhatsApp groups. *"It's fewer cupcakes, Karen."*

◆ ◆ ◆

Signs You're a Wanker Parent
You say "babyccino" with a straight face.
You refer to nap time as "mindfulness practice for toddlers."
You call the park "an outdoor sensory stimulation area."

◆ ◆ ◆

4. Hosting Playdates for Maximum Chaos

Playdates are your chance to impress (and annoy) other parents.

How to Overwhelm Everyone:

Serve *"healthy"* snacks like kale crisps and hummus. Watch the kids cry and refuse to eat.

Plan a *"fun activity"* that requires more effort from the parents than the kids.
  "We're making organic bird feeders out of locally sourced pinecones!"

Insist that every child leaves with a party bag full of artisanal nonsense, like homemade soap or *"gratitude journals."*

Advanced Move:
Hire a photographer to document the playdate. Post the photos

online with captions like, *"Creating magical memories!"*

❖ ❖ ❖

5. The Holiday Show-Off

From Christmas to Halloween, holidays are a chance to show the world just how extra you are.

Wanker Holiday Moves:

Christmas Chaos: Start decorating in October. Dress your entire family in matching pyjamas for a Christmas card photo. Add a newsletter detailing every minor accomplishment of the year.
Birthday Bragging: Throw a themed party with a Pinterest-worthy cake. Insist it's *"for the kids,"* but secretly make it about you.
Halloween Horror: Dress your child as something unnecessarily elaborate, like a hand-sewn dragon costume complete with LED lights. Say, *"Oh, it was just a little DIY project."*

❖ ❖ ❖

The Wanker Parent's Holiday Card Checklist
Brag about little achievements: "Tommy learned to clap this year!"
Mention exotic trips: "We simply adored our week in Santorini."
Use the phrase "We're so blessed." At least twice.

❖ ❖ ❖

6. The Teenager Years: Advanced Wankery

As your mini-wankers grow, your parenting wankery needs to evolve.

How to Annoy Your Teenager:

Show up to parent-teacher meetings with a clipboard, ready to *"discuss opportunities for growth."*
Use slang incorrectly.
  "That outfit is so fire, right? Or is it lit?"
Insist on following them on every social media platform. Comment on all their posts with, *"Looking good, champ!"*

Advanced Move:
Embarrass them in public by loudly referring to yourself as their *"bestie."*

◆ ◆ ◆

Conclusion: Leave a Legacy of Chaos

Raising mini-wankers isn't just about guiding them through life—it's about teaching them to embrace their inner tossery with pride. From overachieving at school drop-offs to dominating playdates and embarrassing them as teens, your parenting style will leave a legacy that's equal parts infuriating and unforgettable.

So go forth, wanker parents. Raise the next generation of chaos-bringers, and remember: if other parents aren't secretly rolling their eyes at you, are you even doing it right?

◆ ◆ ◆

THE SEASONAL WANKER

Chapter Twelve

"Annoying Everyone, One Holiday at a Time"

The changing seasons bring endless opportunities for wankery, and the true seasonal tosser knows how to milk every holiday for maximum annoyance. Whether it's turning Christmas into a competitive sport or stretching Halloween into a month-long spectacle, this chapter will show you how to dominate every season like the wanker you were born to be.

❖ ❖ ❖

1. Christmas Chaos

Christmas is the crown jewel of seasonal wankery—a time to shine brighter than the tackiest tinsel.

How to Be the Ultimate Christmas Tosspot:

Start Early: Put your decorations up in September. Loudly judge anyone who waits until December, saying, *"It's about the spirit of the season!"*
Overdecorate: Turn your house into a beacon visible from space. Inflatable reindeer? Check. Lights that play *Jingle Bells*? Double check.
Matching Pajamas: Force your entire family (including the

dog) into matching Christmas pyjamas for a photo shoot. Post it with the caption:

"So blessed to have these weirdos in my life."

Advanced Move:
Create a Christmas playlist that includes your own off-key recording of *Silent Night.* Insist everyone listens to it during dinner.

❖ ❖ ❖

> *The Wanker's Holiday Card Checklist*
> *Include a family photo where everyone is unnaturally posed.*
> *Add a newsletter that details every minor family achievement.*
> *"Little Timmy learned to tie his shoes this year!"*
> *End with: "Wishing you love and light this holiday season."*

❖ ❖ ❖

2. Valentine's Vomit

Valentine's Day is less about love and more about showing off.

How to Be the Worst on February 14th:

> **The Over-the-Top Gesture:** Send an enormous bouquet of roses to your partner's office. Include a note that says, *"Just a little something for my soulmate."*
> **Social Media Bragging:** Post a photo of the dinner you're "cooking" (actually takeout) with a caption like, *"A romantic evening with my love. #CoupleGoals."*
> **Gifting Nonsense:** Buy something impractical, like lingerie two sizes too small or a box of chocolates shaped like miniature Eiffel Towers.

Advanced Move:
Write an overly sentimental poem and read it aloud in a restaurant. Loudly.

❖ ❖ ❖

The Wanker's Guide to Single Valentine's Day
Post cryptic statuses like, "Love yourself first."
Treat yourself to an overpriced meal and caption it: "Who needs a Valentine when you've got steak?"
Share a meme that says, "It's just a capitalist scam anyway."

❖ ❖ ❖

3. Easter Extraordinaire

Easter isn't just for kids—it's your chance to dominate spring with smugness.

How to Wankerize Easter:

Gourmet Egg Hunt: Organise an Easter egg hunt with imported Belgian chocolates. Tell everyone the store-bought ones are *"bad for the environment."*
Brunch Bragging: Host a pastel-themed brunch with quiche, mimosas, and organic free-range eggs. Insist on calling it a *"celebration of rebirth."*
Instagram Overload: Post a photo of a single daffodil with the caption:
   "Spring reminds us of life's fragility and beauty."

Advanced Move:

Hand-paint your own eggs and act offended when nobody compliments them.

❖ ❖ ❖

4. Summer Shenanigans

Summer is all about barbecues, beach trips, and turning up the heat on your tossery.

How to Dominate the Sunny Season:

The BBQ Dictator: Host a barbecue, but insist on grilling everything yourself. Critique everyone else's technique.

"No, no, you can't flip it yet—it needs to caramelise."

Beach Fashionista: Wear flip-flops everywhere, including places where they're wildly inappropriate (like funerals or job interviews).

Holiday Bragging: Post a photo of your feet on a sun lounger with the caption:

"Work hard, play harder. #BeachLife"

Advanced Move:
Complain about the heat while sunbathing. Loudly announce, *"I'm not complaining, but it's just TOO hot."*

❖ ❖ ❖

5. Autumn Arseholery

Autumn brings crunchy leaves, pumpkin spice lattes, and unparalleled levels of wankery.

How to Be the Ultimate Autumn Tosspot:

Pumpkin Overload: Buy every pumpkin-spiced product you can find, from candles to cereal. Post a photo of your haul with:

"It's officially PSL season!"

Leaf Photographer: Take 37 photos of yourself throwing leaves in the air. Post the best one with the caption:

"Falling for fall."

Halloween Horror: Go overboard with your costume. Insist it's *"an ironic commentary on consumer culture"* when it's just a pirate outfit.

Advanced Move:
Carve a pumpkin that looks like Banksy's *Girl with a Balloon* and call it *"seasonal art."*

❖ ❖ ❖

6. New Year, New Wanker

The calendar might change, but your tossery remains timeless.

How to Ruin New Year's for Everyone:

> **Resolution Evangelist:** Announce all your resolutions loudly and often. *"This is the year I finally go vegan and run a marathon!"* (You won't.)
> **Party Bragger:** Go to an exclusive New Year's party and post a selfie at midnight with:
> *"2025, I'm ready for you! #Blessed"*
> **Firework Critic:** Complain that the fireworks *"lacked artistic vision."*

Advanced Move:
Host a *"Vision Board"* party where everyone has to paste pictures of their goals onto a poster. Act smug about how *"manifestation is so powerful."*

❖ ❖ ❖

Conclusion: Celebrating Wankery Year-Round

Every season is a chance to level up your tossery. From Christmas to Halloween, summer barbecues to Valentine's drama, the key to being a seasonal wanker is to make every holiday just a little bit too much.

So dust off your pumpkin spice mug, dig out your matching Christmas pyjama's, and remember: if someone isn't rolling their eyes at your holiday antics, you're not doing it right.

❖ ❖ ❖

WANKER AT THE WHEEL

Chapter Thirteen

"Driving Like a Wanker, Because Why Not?"

◆ ◆ ◆

The road is a jungle, and every wanker knows it's not about getting from Point A to Point B—it's about asserting your dominance along the way. Whether you're cutting people off, blasting terrible music, or arguing with your sat-nav, this chapter will teach you how to become a driving tosser of legendary proportions.

◆ ◆ ◆

1. Road Rage Rampage

A true wanker thrives on road rage. It's not about solving problems; it's about making sure everyone knows you're angry.

How to Unleash Maximum Rage:

> **The Horn Honk Hero:** Blast your horn at anyone who hesitates for more than half a second at a green light. Bonus points for shouting, *"LEARN TO DRIVE!"* even when you're the one in the wrong lane.
> **The Gesture Guru:** Master the art of aggressive hand gestures. The windshield-wiping motion is a classic.
> **The Tailgate Terror:** Drive so close to the car in front that you're practically in their backseat. Flash your headlights like a lunatic for added effect.

Advanced Move:
When someone overtakes you, speed up to match their pace, then slow down when they try to pass again. It's not petty—it's strategy.

❖ ❖ ❖

> *The Road Rage Wanker's Playlist*
> "Move Bitch" – Ludacris
> "Highway to Hell" – AC/DC
> "Born to Be Wild" – Steppenwolf
> "Shut Up and Drive" – Rihanna
> "Life Is a Highway" – Rascal Flatts

❖ ❖ ❖

2. Parking Lot Prowess

The parking lot is a battlefield, and every wanker knows the best spot isn't just a convenience—it's a trophy.

How to Dominate Parking:

The Space Snatcher: Wait until someone else is about to pull into a spot, then swoop in at the last second. Smile innocently as they fume.
The Bad Angle Bandit: Park diagonally across two spaces, preferably near the entrance. Bonus points for doing this in a compact car.
The Reverse Nightmare: Take three minutes to reverse into a spot while holding up a queue of angry drivers. When you finally succeed, get out and check your spacing dramatically.

Advanced Move:
Leave your shopping cart directly behind someone else's car. Blame it on the wind.

3. The Sat-Nav Saboteur

Sat-navs are supposed to make driving easier, but for wankers, they're another opportunity to stir chaos.

How to Annoy Everyone with Your Sat-Nav:

Ignore it completely and insist you know a *"shortcut."* Get lost. Blame the sat-nav.
Change the voice to something ridiculous, like a pirate or Darth Vader. Act confused when nobody finds it funny.
Shout *"RECALCULATING!"* in sync with the device every time you miss a turn.

Advanced Move:
Argue with the sat-nav out loud, as if it can hear you. *"Left? Are you sure, mate?"*

4. Music Tyranny

Your car, your rules, your playlist. Passengers don't get a vote.

How to Annoy with Music:

The Repeat Offender: Play the same song on loop for the entire journey. *"It's a vibe, trust me."*
The Volume Maniac: Crank the music up at traffic lights so loud the bass rattles nearby windows.
The Mood Destroyer: Switch from heavy metal to *Celine Dion* without warning. Insist it's *"all about balance."*

Advanced Move:
Force everyone to listen to your niche podcast about the history of paperclips. Refuse to acknowledge their suffering.

◆ ◆ ◆

The Wanker's Driving Mixtape Must-Haves
A guilty pleasure song (e.g., "Barbie Girl")
A song you pretend to like for "cred" ("Bohemian Rhapsody")
A song nobody likes but you insist is "underrated" ("Crazy Frog")

5. Passenger Problems

The only thing worse than a backseat driver is a wanker driver. Make sure your passengers know exactly who's in charge.

Techniques for Maximum Passenger Annoyance:

Refuse to adjust the air conditioning. *"It's my car, my climate."*
Accelerate suddenly whenever someone is trying to drink or eat.
Provide unsolicited driving advice to anyone else in the car, even if they're just sitting there.
   "You really should check your blind spots more, Gemma."

Advanced Move:
Claim you're out of petrol halfway through the trip. Pull over dramatically and make everyone pitch in for gas money.

6. The School Run Show-Off

For parents, the school run is prime wanker time.

How to Dominate the Drop-Off Zone:

Arrive 15 minutes early and park in the loading zone.
Play classical music loudly to show your superior taste.
Get out of the car in your athleisure outfit to suggest you're heading to Pilates (you're not).

Advanced Move:
Rev your engine unnecessarily as you leave, ensuring everyone hears you. *"It's just the exhaust—it's meant to sound like that."*

7. The Holiday Road Trip Wanker

Road trips are the Olympics of driving tossery. Prepare accordingly.

How to Annoy Everyone on a Road Trip:

Overpack the car with pointless items like three yoga mats and a portable juicer.

Refuse to stop at fast food joints, insisting on finding *"a cute little café"* that takes an hour to locate.

Take constant detours to see *"hidden gems"* that turn out to be underwhelming fields.

Advanced Move:

Plan the entire route to avoid motorways *"because the scenic route is just so much better."* Add two hours to the journey.

◆ ◆ ◆

Conclusion: Honk If You're a Wanker

Driving is more than just a way to get around—it's a lifestyle. Whether you're terrorising the parking lot, blasting questionable music, or arguing with your sat-nav, the goal is to make every journey memorable (for everyone, not just you).

So buckle up, hit the accelerator, and remember: you're not just driving—you're performing. Honk if you're fabulous.

◆ ◆ ◆

AFTERWORD

"In Defense of Wankery"

And there you have it: the complete, unapologetic guide to embracing life as a wanker. If you've made it this far, congratulations—you're either a seasoned tosser or well on your way to becoming one. Either way, you're in excellent company.

But let's take a moment to reflect (because wankers *love* to reflect, ideally while staring pensively out a window). This book wasn't just about offering terrible advice, stirring chaos, or celebrating pettiness—though it's done plenty of that. It's also about celebrating the quirks, contradictions, and ridiculousness that make us human.

Being a wanker isn't necessarily a bad thing. It's about leaning into your eccentricities, unapologetically owning your quirks, and finding joy in life's absurdities. It's about laughing at yourself, annoying your friends, and sometimes—just sometimes—forcing everyone to listen to your niche podcast about the history of spoons.

So, whether you're sending passive-aggressive emails, hogging the gym equipment, or arguing with your sat-nav about the best route to the pub, remember this: the world would be unbearably dull without wankers like us. We keep things interesting. We make people laugh, roll their eyes, and occasionally question their life choices. And, honestly, isn't that a legacy worth leaving?

Thank you for joining me on this ridiculous journey. Now go forth, embrace your inner wanker, and continue to make life a little more interesting—one eye roll at a time.

Yours in unrepentant wankery,
Sir Knobulous W. Pompington

A NOTE ON THE COVER DESIGN

The book cover:

If a wanker were a colour, it would undoubtedly be **chartreuse**—that obnoxious yellow-green shade that screams, *"I'm bold, I'm loud, and I'm definitely not for everyone."*

Why chartreuse?

It's flashy without being classy, much like a wanker at a club in sunglasses.
It's polarising—people either love it or loathe it, just like wankers.
It's the colour equivalent of ordering a half-oat, half-soy caramel macchiato with extra foam: unnecessarily complicated.

The book cover text:

Hot Pink: Bold, brash, and not afraid to stand out (even when it shouldn't).

PRAISE FOR AUTHOR

A literary genius. Or at least he thinks so. This book is a masterclass in being insufferable—perfect for the wanker in all of us.

- THE WANKER TIMES

Sir Knobulous is like the Shakespeare of petty nonsense. His words are so sharp, they could cut through a vegan's excuse for eating cheese.

- KAREN T. COMPLAINER, AUTHOR OF HOW TO ALWAYS BE RIGHT

This book made me laugh so hard, I almost spilled my oat latte. Almost.

- JASPER VON ARROGANCE, INFLUENCER AND PROFESSIONAL TOSSPOT

I read this cover to cover, and now my coworkers won't speak to me. Mission accomplished.

- CHAD FLEXINGTON, CORPORATE BUZZWORD SPECIALIST

If you've ever clapped when a plane landed, this book will make you feel seen.

- DELILAH SELFRIGHTEOUS, EDITOR-IN-CHIEF, PRETENTIOUS MONTHLY

Absolutely brilliant. Except for the parts that aren't, which is most of them.

- BARRY FROM ACCOUNTING

A waste of paper and ink. But oddly compelling.

- SOME RANDOM BLOKE ON TWITTER

I didn't read it, but I love the cover.

- MY FRIEND WHO BUYS BOOKS BUT NEVER OPENS THEM